MONSTER HEROES

ZOMBIES AND MEATBALLS

BY BLAKE HOENA
ILLUSTRATED BY DAVE BARDIN

Raintree is an imprint of Capstone Global Library Limited, a company incorporated in England and Wales having its registered office at 264 Banbury Road, Oxford, OX2 7DY – Registered company number: 6695582

www.raintree.co.uk
myorders@raintree.co.uk
Text © Capstone Global Library Limited 2017
The moral rights of the proprietor have been asserted.

Edited by Christianne Jones
Designed by Ted Williams
Original illustrations © 2017
Illustrated by Dave Bardin
Production by Katy LaVigne
Originated by Capstone Press
Printed and bound in China

ISBN 978 1 4747 2781 5
20 19 18 17 16
10 9 8 7 6 5 4 3 2 1

British Library Cataloguing in Publication Data
A full catalogue record for this book is available from
the British Library.

Photo credits: Shutterstock: kasha_malasha, design element, popular business, design element

CONTENTS

Mina thinks people taste like dirty socks, so beet juice is her snack of choice. Its red color has fooled her parents into thinking that she's a traditional blood-sucking vampire instead of a superhero hopeful. She has the ability to change into a bat or a mouse at will.

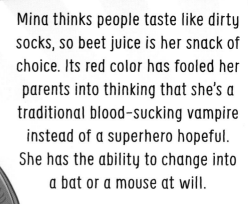

Brian is the brainy one amongst his friends. Unlike other zombies, Brian prefers tofu to brains. No matter what sort of trouble is brewing, Brian always comes up with a plan to save the day, like a true superhero.

BRIAN *(the Zombie)*

WILL (the Ghost)

Will is quite shy. Luckily he can turn invisible any time he wants because he is a ghost. When Will is doing good deeds, he likes to remain unseen. His invisibility helps him act brave like a real superhero.

With a wave of her wand and a poetic chant, Linda can reverse any magical curse. She hopes to use her magic to help people, just like a superhero would.

LINDA (the Witch)

BRAINS OR BRIAN?

Brian was at his desk working when he heard a strange noise.

"*Braaaiiins!*" came a loud moan.

Brian glanced around his room.

"Did someone just say my name?" Brian whispered.

"*Braaaiiins!*" came the moan again. Only this time, it was louder.

Brian looked up from his homework. He was getting annoyed. He was also getting a little scared.

"Who keeps calling my name?" he asked out loud.

His friends were always saying he studied too much. Maybe they were outside trying to scare him.

"Knock it off you guys," Brian said. "I'm trying to study."

When the moaning continued, Brian realised it wasn't his friends. He went over to his window and looked outside. What he saw scared him more than the moaning.

"Oh, no!" he gasped.

Zombies were everywhere! Hundreds of them lumbered and stumbled about. They destroyed everything in their path, including plants, trees and mailboxes.

"*Braaaiiins*!" they moaned.

Brian knew that a horde of hungry zombies could be a danger to anyone with a brain.

"*Braaaiiins*!" they moaned louder.

"They are saying '*Braaaiiins*' not '*Briiiaaan,*'" Brian said. "It's true what people say about zombies – they really are hard to understand!"

Brian needed to take action, and he had to do it fast.

He made his way downstairs and peeked outside. More and more zombies filled the streets.

"What is going on?" Brian asked quietly. "The other zombies are usually so well behaved."

"*Braaaiiins!*" they moaned.

Then Brian saw the problem.

Down the road was Tofu Brains Deli & Coffee Shop. A CLOSED sign hung outside.

"That's it! They are all hungry!" Brian said.

"*Braaaiiins!*" the zombies moaned.

"I need to call my friends," Brian said. "We need to meet at our hideout right away!"

WHERE ARE THE BRAINS?

Brian's friends were not like other monsters. They did not hurt or scare people. Brian's friends helped people.

They used their special monster powers for good. They wanted to be like superheroes and save the day.

Brian lumbered to the cemetery and climbed up to the hideout. His friends were already there.

Mina hung upside down in one corner. Will floated in another corner. Linda sat in a chair with her pet caterpillar sitting on her shoulder.

"What's wrong?" Linda asked.

"The Tofu Brain Deli & Coffee Shop closed," Brian said.

"No way!" Mina shouted. "I loved that place."

"So did I, but why is that such a big problem?" Will asked. "There are other places to eat."

"But that's where all the zombies eat. Now they are hungry," Brian said. "They are forming a horde."

His friend's eyes went wide with fear. Sure, zombies were slow and clumsy. But a horde of them was unstoppable. They would eat and destroy everything in their path.

"They will look for anyone or anything with a brain," Brian said. "And then . . ."

"This IS a big problem!" Will said.

"It sure is!" Brian said.

Mina held up a map of the city.

"Where do you think they will go?" she asked.

"That's easy," Brian said. "Victor Frankenstein Primary School has the most brains in town."

Brian looked at the map. He put a finger on Zombie Town. Then he traced the streets leading to the primary school.

"This is the path they will follow," Brian said.

"How do we stop the horde from getting there?" Will asked.

Brian studied the map. There were stops and restaurants along the way to the school.

"That's it!" Brian said.

"What's it?" Linda asked.

"A trip to the meatball shop, that's what!" Brian said.

"Getting a bite to eat?" Mina said. "That's your brilliant plan?"

"Just trust me," Brian said.

MEATBALL BRAINS

The friends stood outside Randy's Meatball Sandwich Shop.

"The meatballs here are really good," Will said.

"And they kind of look like little brains," Brian said, holding one up. "Now, huddle up, team!"

Brian whispered his plan. They all agreed and got into position.

Linda waved her wand at the restaurant's sign.

"Your name must change," she chanted.

Poof! The sign now read Igor's Meatball Brainwich Shop. Linda's job was done.

Now it was Brian's turn. He joined the zombie horde.

"*Braaaiiins!*" the zombies moaned as they lumbered down the street.

"*Meeeatbaaalls!*" Brian groaned.

"*Braaaiiins!*" the zombies moaned again.

"*Meeeatbaaalls!*" Brian groaned louder.

The zombies kept moaning. Brian kept groaning louder. Soon, the zombies' moans changed to groans. Brian's job was done.

"*Meeeatbaaalls!*" the zombies groaned.

Will tied a string to a meatball. Then he took off his sheet. Now he was invisible.

Will used the meatball on a string to lead the zombies to the sandwich shop. Will pulled the meatball away as soon as the zombies reached for it.

"*Meeeatbaaalls!*" the zombies groaned.

Brian groaned along with them. "*Meeeatbaaalls!*"

Brian and the zombies followed Will right to the restaurant. Will's job was done. Now it was Mina's turn to take over.

Mina quickly made stacks and stacks of meatball sandwiches. Then she changed into a bat. She fluttered about the restaurant.

The horde of zombies entered the shop and attacked the piles of meatball sandwiches.

"*Meeeatbaaalls*!" the zombies groaned.

The friends regrouped outside the sub shop. They watched as the zombies ate every sandwich in sight.

"We stopped them!" Linda said.

"The monster heroes saved the day again," Mina said.

"That's because we make a great team," Brian said.

"We sure do," Will mumbled between bites. "What? Nobody else is hungry?"

DAVE BARDIN

Dave Bardin studied illustration at Cal State Fullerton while working as an art teacher. As an artist, Dave has worked on many different projects for television, books, comics and animation. In his spare time Dave enjoys watching documentaries, listening to podcasts, traveling and spending time with friends and family. He works in Los Angeles, California.

BLAKE A. HOENA

Blake A. Hoena grew up in central Wisconsin, USA, where he wrote stories about robots conquering the moon and trolls lumbering around the woods behind his parents house. He now lives in Minnesota, USA, and continues to write about fun things like space aliens and superheroes. Blake has written more than fifty chapter books and graphic novels for children.

ZOMBIE'S GLOSSARY

brain zombie snack; also, the organ in a person's head that controls bodily functions and is used for thinking

cemetery hang-out for zombies; also, a place where dead people are buried

hideout secret place

horde large group of people (or zombies)

lumber to move in a slow, awkward way; the only way zombies move

tofu food made from soybeans, often used as a meat substitute (this has nothing to do with zombies)

THINK ABOUT IT

1. Why do you think the author chose to name the main zombie Brian, which is spelt almost the same as "brain"?

2. Within this story, several place names are used, such as Zombie Town and Frankenstein Primary School. How does including these names help the setting of the story?

3. Each of the characters plays a part in the plan to stop the horde of zombies. What would have happened if one of the characters failed to do their part?

WRITE ABOUT IT

1. What would you do if you saw a horde of zombies? Make a list describing your plan.

2. Zombies are not pretty creatures. Write a detailed description of a zombie, and use at least five character traits.

3. The story ends with the zombies happily eating meatball sandwiches. What happens when they get hungry again? Write a paragraph about what you think will happen.